Let's Play at the Playground!

Pat Rumbaugh, The Play Lady

written by Pat Rumbaugh
photographs by Daniel Nakamura

LET'S PLAY AT THE PLAYGROUND!

Copyright © 2012 by Community Voice Media, LLC

Community Voice Media, LLC.
CVM

PO Box 564, Round Hill, VA 20142
www.communityvoicemedia.com

Library of Congress Control Number: 2012905020

ISBN: 978-0-9776613-6-7

Printed in China

Foreword

Playgrounds are beautiful places that add laughter and joy to our world. They provide a space where kids can learn to run, jump and swing. Children learn how to negotiate with and respect each other through the interactions that take place on playgrounds. Kids who play grow up to "play" better as adults.

This book captures the simple, but important, spirit and energy of children at play through joyous, beautiful photographs. None of these children are smiling for the camera. They're smiling because they're experiencing one of life's most basic pleasures – the freedom to play.

Through play, children can lead happier, fitter, smarter and more socially adept and creative lives. I hope that this book inspires the children and parents reading it to go out and play.

Darell Hammond
CEO and Co-Founder of KaBOOM!

KaBOOM! is the national non-profit that works to bring play back into the lives of all children. KaBOOM!, advocates the importance of each child having a safe and engaging place, as well as the time, to play.

Climbing
is an adventure!

Jumping
is like flying!

Running

feels great!

Sliding
is fun!

Swinging
makes me smile!

Climb
with me!

Jump
with me!

Run
with me!

Slide

with me!

Swing
with me!

Climb
together!

Jump
together!

Run
together!

Slide
together!

Swing
together!

Play together!

Pat Rumbaugh, The Play Lady and Founder of Takoma Plays, was a physical education teacher at the Washington International School for more than 25 years. In 2009 the Washington Post named her "All-Met Girls Tennis Coach of the Year." She is a passionate play advocate.

Daniel Nakamura lives in Silver Spring, MD with his wife Erin and daughter Emily. He is a professional photographer and owns Booth-o-Rama Photobooths which serves the Washington, D.C. metro region. He loves to document kids in action and promotes play through his photography.